a Dragon

teeth

backs

legs

wings

tails

To our grandson, Noah

BEACH LANE BOOKS
An imprint of Simon & Schuster Children's Publishing Division
1230 Avenue of the Americas, New York, New York 10020
Copyright © 2015 by Douglas Florian
BEACH LANE BOOKS is a trademark of Simon & Schuster, Inc.
For information about special discounts for bulk purchases, please contact Simon &
Schuster Special Sales at 1-866-506-1949 or business@simonandschuster.com.
The Simon & Schuster Speakers Bureau can bring authors to your live event. For more
information or to book an event, contact the Simon & Schuster Speakers Bureau at
1-866-248-3049 or visit our website at www.simonspeakers.com.
Book design by Ann Bobco
The text for this book is set in Grandma.
The illustrations for this book are rendered in mixed media.
Manufactured in China
0115 SCP
First Edition
10 9 8 7 6 5 4 3 2 1
Library of Congress Cataloging-in-Publication Data
Florian, Douglas, author, illustrator.
How to draw a dragon / Douglas Florian.—First edition.
p. cm.
Summary: Illustrations and easy-to-read, rhyming text guide the reader in drawing scaly,
knobby-kneed dragons that fly, play musical instruments, ride bicycles, and more.
ISBN 978-1-4424-7399-7 (hardcover)
ISBN 978-1-4424-7400-0 (eBook)
[1. Stories in rhyme. 2. Dragons—Fiction. 3. Drawing—Fiction. 4. Humorous stories.]
I. Title.
PZ8.3.F66How 2015
[E]—dc23
2014012062

How to Draw
a Dragon

DOUGLAS FLORIAN

BEACH LANE BOOKS   New York   London   Toronto   Sydney   New Delhi

Drawing dragons isn't hard.
Drag a dragon to your yard.

Dragons may be large in size.

You'll need lots of art supplies.

Dragons, when they wake, are grumpy.

And their heads are rather bumpy.

Careful when you draw each claw.

Dragons _also_ love to draw!

Draw your dragon's pointed spines

using lots of jagged lines.

While your dragon's laying eggs,

take the time to draw her legs.

Dragons have large, knobby knees.

And it rains when dragons sneeze!

While you both ride on your bike,

you can draw your dragon's spike.

Draw your dragon's wings in flight,

Draw your dragon's bearded chin

while he plays the violin.

as she's watching dragonflies.

Dragon fire has reds and yellows,

and it's good to toast

marshmallows.

Time for dragons now

to fly.

Give a hug . . .

then wave good-bye.

All those dragons had to go . . .

but your drawing's . . .

in a show!

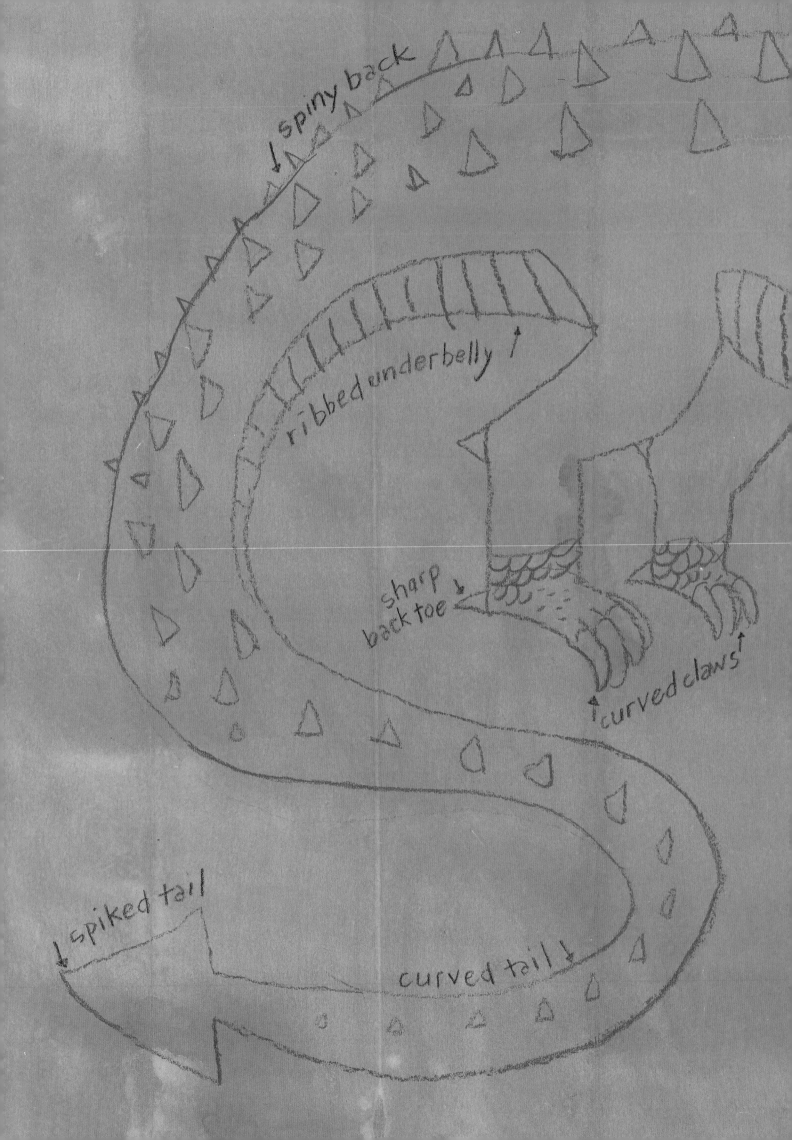